D0989728

You are enough!

A. L. Murphy

MARION CARNEGIE LIBRARY
206 SOUTH MARKET
Marion, IL 62959

The Warrior Princess

Dedicated to Jesse, John David, Nick & David Lee

ILLUSTRATED BY
Jan Shannon and D.L. Murphy

Settle in my yogi friends and truth seekers.

This is the tale of

The Warrior Princess.

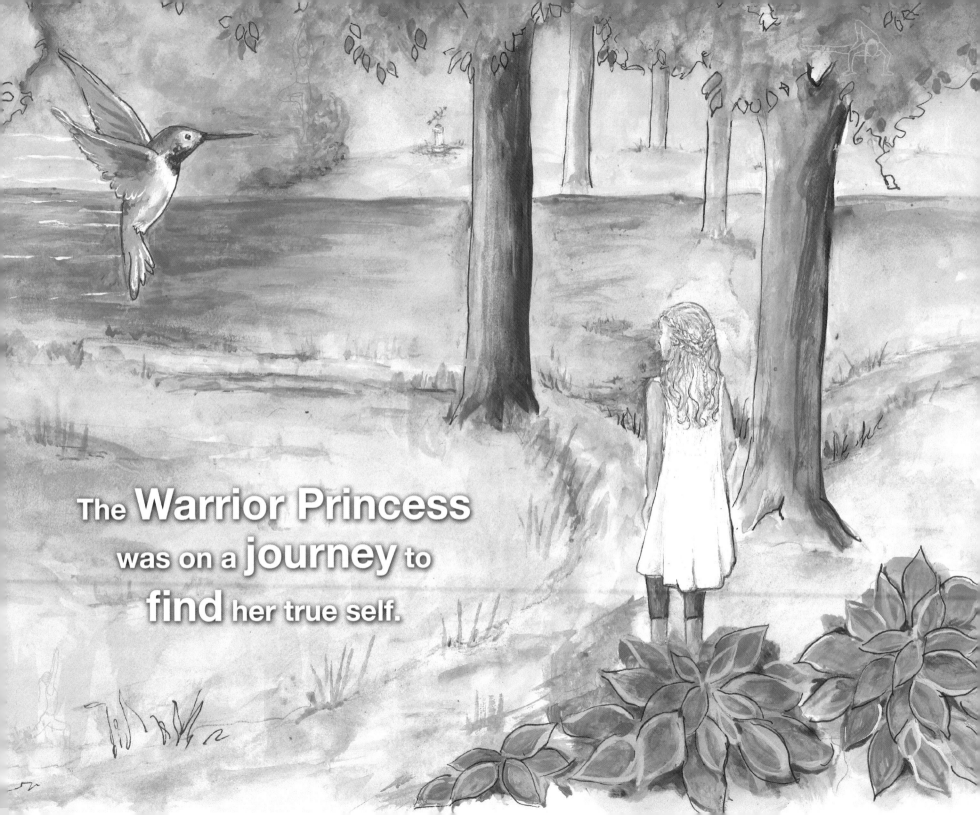

The **Warrior Princess** was on a **journey** to **find** her true self.

She looked everywhere.
She asked everyone.

Who am I?

And
the world
told her.

The giraffe said,

"You're too short."

The frog said,

"I'm a beautiful green, you're **not the right color.**"

The peacock said,

"Look how **beautiful** my feathers are."

"You're
not
as
pretty
as me."

So she felt **ugly** and **afraid** they were right.

But she was the **Warrior Princess**
and so she pushed on, knowing that
their answers did not exactly feel right.
It was **not** her **truth**.

She had heard that when
you know who **you** are,
you will **feel** content.

The **Warrior Princess** journeyed on.
She came to a **secret** door hidden along a stone wall.

She noticed a **key** in the lock.

She turned the **key,** pressed the door **open,**

and
stepped
inside
to find a
beautiful
garden.

In the **garden** there were trees to climb,

flowers with wonderful scents and **happy,** frolicking animals.

In the middle of the **garden** there was a large tree and beneath it, a regal and **wise**, old Lion. She sensed from just his presence that he alone could help her **discover** the **truth**.

Though lions are ferocious,
in his presence, she was **not afraid**.

She approached the Lion and asked,

"Who am I?"

The Lion told her as he had told all

the creatures of the forests,

"**Journey** to the lake and when you get there,

peer into the water and you will find

the **answer** to your question."

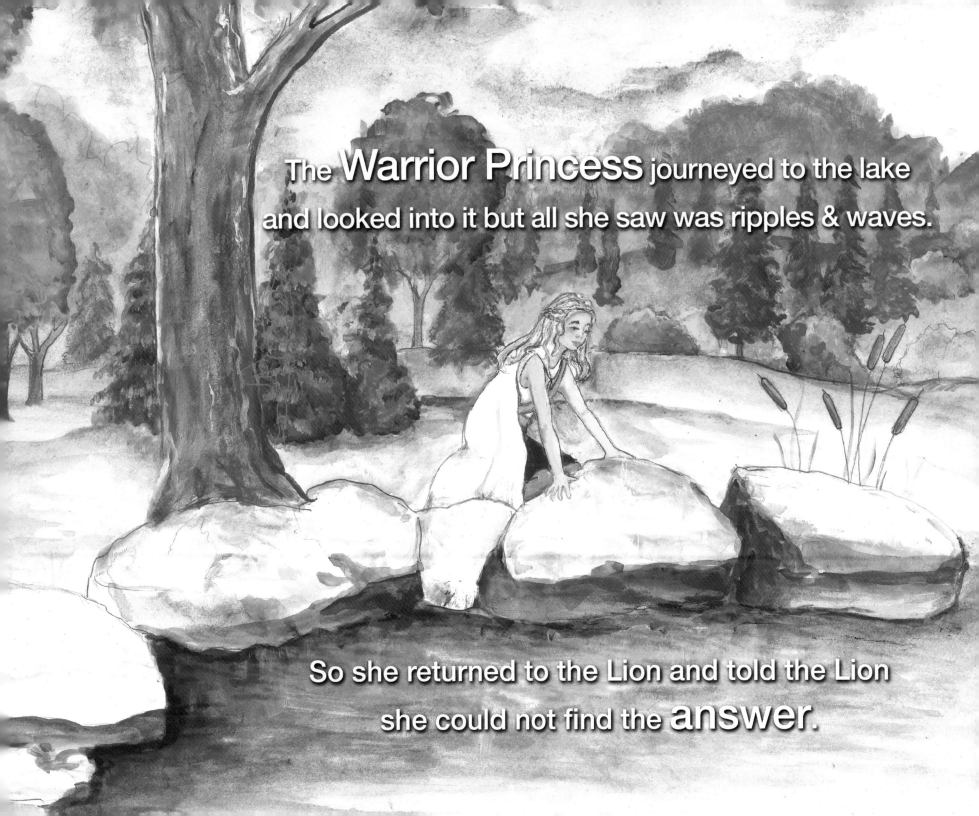

The **Warrior Princess** journeyed to the lake and looked into it but all she saw was ripples & waves.

So she returned to the Lion and told the Lion she could not find the **answer**.

The Lion
replied,
"Oh My child,
but you can.

The waves and ripples are obstacles
keeping you from seeing your true self.
You must remove the obstacles and still your mind."

"How can I remove the obstacles?" she asked.

The wise old Lion told her she must place each **obstacle** on a cloud and let it **sail** away. Then she will have the answer to the question,

"**Who am I?**"

The **Warrior Princess**
returned to the water's edge and as she sat,
she closed her eyes and placed
each of the **obstacles** in her **life** on a cloud
and **blew** the cloud away.

FEAR

Her first obstacle was fear.

She placed fear on a cloud and whispered

" I am brave "

and as she exhaled

the cloud sailed away.

The second obstacle
was huge and it was
an **ugly** tangle of the
"I'm **not** enoughs."

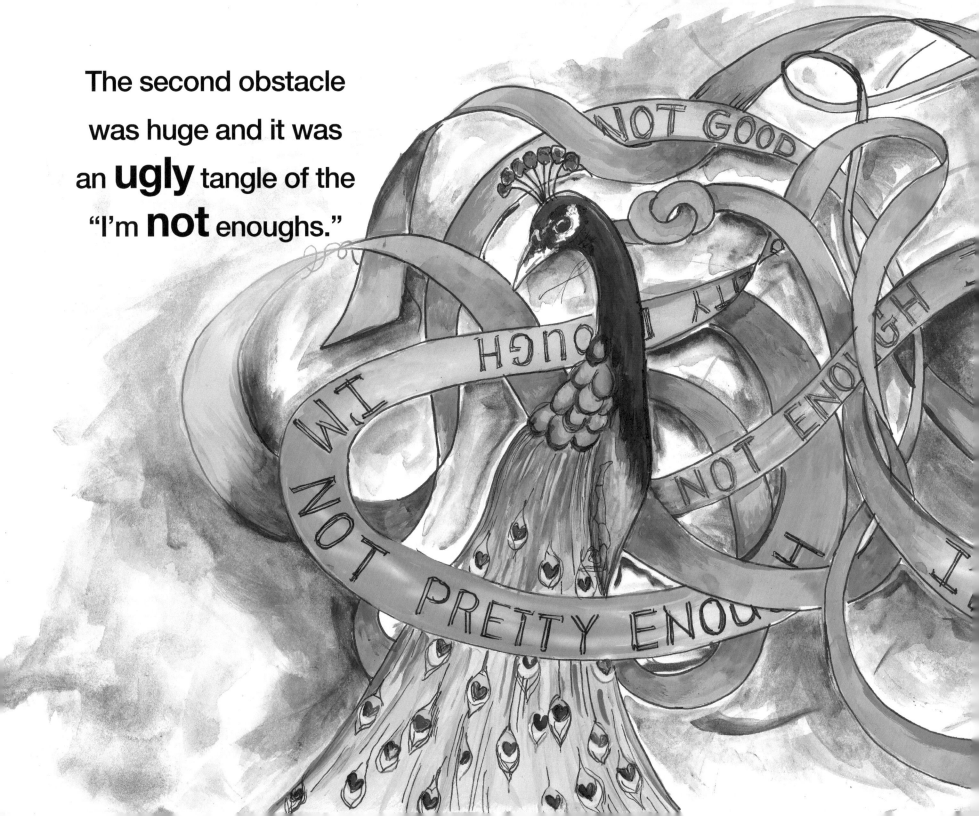

I'm **not pretty** enough,
I'm **not tall** enough,
I'm **not smart** enough,
I'm **not good** enough,
I'm **not** the **right** color.

In her mind, she placed the huge tangle of **"I'm not enoughs"** on a cloud and as she did, she said aloud,

"I am strong, I AM ENOUGH," and the words pushed the cloud away.

Her mind became still. It was clear and peaceful.
She felt the peace in her body. She felt the peace in her heart.

The **Warrior Princess** was now ready to peer into the lake. The once rough surface was smooth like a glass mirror.

She looked
deeply into it
and **smiled.**

Now, my young friends,
take a moment to ponder.

Don't answer out loud.
Close your **eyes**, still your **mind**,
and **see** what comes to you.

So I ask you,
what do **you think** she saw?

The Warrior Princess

D. L. Murphy is a certified adult/children's yoga instructor and has a master's degree in Early Childhood Education and Administration. She received her bachelor's degree in Economics and Fine Arts from Vanderbilt University. The Warrior Princess is her first children's book to author and illustrate. Home is a farm in Franklin, Tennessee where she resides with her husband and family.

THE ILLUSTRATORS

D.L Murphy teamed up with Nashville artist Jan Shannon to create the artwork in this book. Their collaborative effort focused on an interactive design meant to engage children in reading or listening, looking and exploring. The story comes alive with colorful characters in beautiful landscapes and playful sub-story imagery.

Jan Shannon studied art at Volunteer State Community College and O'More School of Design. In addition to this book, Jan illustrated "Mason the Lucky Dog" in 2016. Other works include Heritage Quilt Barn murals across rural Tennessee. She lives with her husband, Robby, and has two grown children, Brooke and Adam.

THE DESIGNER

Jackie Bradley-Rippey served as our advisory and design guru. She is an international award winning designer living with Lola, her rescue Aussie Cattle Dog.

ACKNOWLEDGEMENTS

Mira Benson (Global Family Yoga) whose encouragement to make this story into a children's book lit the fire and whose skill with children is an inspiration.

Heather Seagraves, yoga instructor extraordinaire, (Heather Seagraves Somatics) who first affirmed that each of us, unique as we are, is ENOUGH.

Pastor Mike Glenn (Brentwood Baptist Church) whose sermon on knowing who you are served in part as inspiration for this story.

Lynley McMillan who patiently served as our Warrior Princess model.

More than a story of positive affirmation of self-worth, the intent of this book is a springboard for open-ended conversation (What do you think she saw and why?), interactive activities in the vein of ISpy, while also serving as an introduction into the self empowering world of yoga.

For activity suggestions and to tell us what YOU think she saw, visit Kingslandtales.com

Yoga Pose Bank

Name	Sanscrit	Sanscrit Pronunciation
Peacock	Pincha Mayurasana	*peen cha my your ross sin ah*
Lion	Simhasana	*seem hoss sin ah*
Cobra	Bhujangasana	*boo john goss sin ah*
Tree	Vrksasana	*vrick shaw sin ah*
Butterfly	Baddha Konasana	*badda cone nos sin ah*
Frog	Bhekasana	*bay coss sin ah*
Bear	Merudandasana	*mare roo don das sin ah*
Lotus Flower	Padmasana	*pod ma sin ah*
Swan	Hamsasana	*han saw sin ah*
Bridge	Setu Bandhasana	*set two bond das sin ah*
Hummingbird	Maksikanagasana	*mak see can nah goss sin ah*
Warrior I	Virabhadrasana I	*vera bah dra sin ah won*
Giraffe	Parivrtta Prasarita Padottanasana	*parry vrita pras sa rita pod doe ten nos sin ah*
Fox	Adho Muka Svanasana (downward facing dog)	*odd hoe moo kah svan nos sin ah*

San Culpa
A positive word or phrase that is repeated often to oneself for the purpose of motivation and/or encouragement. Ex., "I am strong. I am brave. I am enough."
Culpa means vow. San refers to a connection with the highest truth.

Dristi
A focal point or focused gaze. Something, be it as simple as a spot on a wall, to focus your mind on while letting everything else fade into the background.

CAN YOU FIND THE 51 YOGA POSES HIDDEN WITHIN THE PAGES OF THIS STORY?
Some pages have one, some none, and others have more than one. Look closely and try to find them all.
For example, look in the clouds near the butterfly at the end of the story.

COPYRIGHT © 2018 by D.L. Murphy
All rights reserved. No part of this publication may be reproduced, stored in a retrieval system, or transmitted,
in any form or by any means, electronic, mechanical, photocopying, recording, or otherwise, without written permission from the publisher.

CPSIA information can be obtained at www.ICGtesting.com
Printed in the USA
LVIW010751030219
605256LV00007B/5

9 781732 965805